A Ghost for
Miss Grimscuttle

A Ghost for Miss Grimscuttle

by Jo Furminger

Illustrated by Sally Holmes

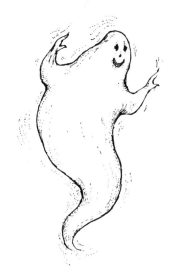

HODDER AND STOUGHTON
LONDON SYDNEY AUCKLAND TORONTO

Also by Jo Furminger

A SPELL FOR MISS GRIMS...

MRS BOFFY'S BIRTHDAY

OH NO, AUNT BELLADO...

A PONY AT BLACKBIRD COTTAGE

BLACKBIRDS' PONY TREK

BLACKBIRDS AND THE GIFT PONY

BLACKBIRDS' OWN GYMKHANA

SADDLE UP, BLACKBIRDS!

BLACKBIRDS AT THE GALLOP

BLACKBIRDS RIDE A MYSTERY TRAIL

British Library Cataloguing in Publication Data
Furminger, Jo
  A ghost for Miss Grimscuttle. – (Leapfrog books)
  I. Title
823'.914[J]   PZ7

ISBN 0-340-32995-5

First published 1983
Second impression 1984

Published by Hodder and Stoughton Children's Books,
a division of Hodder and Stoughton Ltd, Mill Road,
Dunton Green, Sevenoaks, Kent TN13 2YJ

Photoset by Rowland Phototypesetting Ltd,
Bury St Edmunds, Suffolk

Printed in Great Britain by St Edmundsbury Press,
Bury St Edmunds, Suffolk

Contents

Chapter One

THE LOVELY HOUSE

One day Miss Grimscuttle was out for a drive in the country, when all of a sudden she stopped the car and stared.

'Oh, what a lovely house!' breathed Miss Grimscuttle. 'It's exactly what I have always wanted – a big, old, rambling place with lots of tall chimneys and roses round the door!'

The leaded windows seemed to wink invitingly at her in the sunshine, and what was more, there was a sign in the garden saying 'FOR SALE'.

So Miss Grimscuttle turned the car round and headed into town without delay.

'Ah yes,' murmured Mr Slick the estate agent, escorting Miss Grimscuttle to a seat. 'Blackberry Farmhouse, a most charming property. And going for a mere snip!'

'Why?' demanded Miss Grimscuttle, instantly suspicious. 'Has it got dry rot?'

'Oh no, not at all,' Mr Slick assured her, vigorously shaking his head.

'Woodworm?' asked Miss Grimscuttle sharply.

'No, no, nothing like that,' said Mr Slick with a slightly uncomfortable grin.

'Rising damp?'

'Not a hint of damp anywhere,' stammered Mr Slick.

'Death Watch beetle?' pursued Miss Grimscuttle.

'No, no, no, dear lady! The entire house is quite structurally sound, I assure you!'

'Then why is it so CHEAP?' demanded Miss Grimscuttle. 'And why hasn't somebody bought it ALREADY?'

Mr Slick's smile vanished. His face grew pale. His eyes became solemn, and throwing a nervous glance over his shoulder he leaned forward and said in a whisper, 'W-well, you see, it's got a —'

'Very large garden,' interrupted Miss Grimscuttle. 'It doesn't matter to me, young man. I am not afraid of hard work. Go on!'

'It has also got —'

'A range of rather dilapidated outbuildings,' said Miss Grimscuttle. 'Don't worry, I intend to take up spinning and wine-making and other country crafts, so they will come in most useful. But you haven't told me yet why nobody has bought Blackberry Farmhouse?'

Mr Slick took a deep breath and said in an extra loud voice, 'Several people have reported seeing —'

'Scrumpers in the orchard,' finished Miss Grimscuttle. 'Well, I shall soon see *them* off, I can tell you!' She rose to her feet. 'And since you have failed to give me any good reason why I should not buy Blackberry Farmhouse, you may make arrangements straight away. I shall move in there next week.'

Chapter Two

MISS GRIMSCUTTLE MOVES IN

Miss Grimscuttle was as good as her word and the very next week the big removal van packed with all her belongings drew up outside the front door. The men started carrying everything in and Miss Grimscuttle was there to make sure it was all put in the right place.

'Now, that chair goes in the big sitting-room, overlooking the garden!' she shrieked, scurrying round like an anxious hen. 'And that table goes in the kitchen, and that lamp goes in the dining room, and that bed goes upstairs – '

'Where does she *think* we're going to put a bed? In the coalhouse?' grumbled Guy under his breath.

'I wish she'd mind her own blinking business
and keep out of the way till we ask her,' puffed
Charles. 'I nearly dropped the piano on her foot a
minute ago!'

But it was no good. Miss Grimscuttle simply
would not leave them alone until the very last bit
of furniture had been put down. Then, while
Charles and Guy got their breaths back, she
stood and admired the result. All of a sudden her
smile of satisfaction turned to a fierce frown.

'I thought I asked you to put the rocking chair
over *there*,' snapped Miss Grimscuttle, pointing
to an empty spot by the fireplace. Guy stared and
scratched his head.

'But I did!' he said, puzzled.

'Then how,' demanded Miss Grimscuttle, 'do you explain the fact that it is now standing under the window?'

'I – I – ' said Guy, bewildered.

'Chairs don't walk!' pursued Miss Grimscuttle, and she looked so annoyed that Guy and Charles were very glad when the telephone suddenly began to ring and Miss Grimscuttle hurried out into the hall to answer it.

'Phew, I thought we was going to get a right telling-off then,' muttered Charles, wiping his brow.

'Me too!' exclaimed Guy. 'She's really – ' He broke off, grabbing Charles' arm. 'Hey, look – look at that!'

Charles looked. His mouth dropped open. Guy's eyebrows shot upwards into his hair. Because something was happening to the table lamp. Somehow or other it had lifted itself up into the air and was hovering, like a dragon-fly, above the piano. Then right in front of their horrified gaze, it began to move very slowly towards the two removal men.

'G – g – golly!' croaked Guy, finding his voice at last. 'I've just remembered, we've got another job right over the other side of town, and we're ten minutes late already!'

'Y – yes, you're right!' squeaked Charles, struggling to move his feet which somehow seemed to have got glued to the floor. And together they made a rush for the door, almost getting wedged in side by side in their frantic anxiety to get away.

Chapter Three

A NUMBER OF PROBLEMS

Wondering who on earth it could be, Miss Grimscuttle picked up the phone.

'Hallo? Blackberry Farmhouse, Miss Grimscuttle speaking,' she said briskly.

'Brrrrrrrrr,' said the phone, which is all that they ever say when there is nobody on the other end of the line.

With an exclamation of annoyance Miss Grimscuttle slammed down the receiver and strode back. And it didn't take her very long to realise that Charles and Guy had gone without even letting her know.

'Well!' exclaimed Miss Grimscuttle. 'Of all the impudence! But at least it saved me having to give them a tip.'

The thought pleased her so much that she didn't even mind moving the rocking chair all on her own, back into its proper spot by the fire-

place. She pulled and tugged and pushed, and had just got it arranged to her liking when she turned round and her hair positively frizzled with anger. Because instead of being against the wall, her writing desk was now slap bang in the middle of the room!

'Oh, this is just too much!' howled Miss Grimscuttle. Why on earth couldn't those wretched removal men have done their job properly? For two pins she would fetch them back, if only she knew where they had gone! Meanwhile, it would be quicker to put the writing desk back herself.

Puffing, panting and muttering under her breath, Miss Grimscuttle inched the heavy desk, one corner at a time, against the wall. As soon as she was satisfied that everything was exactly right, she marched into the kitchen to make herself a cup of tea.

But she was only half-way there when she suddenly had the strangest feeling. As if – well, as if – somebody was *following* her. Not only that, but Miss Grimscuttle fancied, just *fancied*, that from the corner of her eye she had seen something move. She whirled round and glared.

There was nobody there.

'I hope there are no stray cats prowling around after scraps,' grumbled Miss Grimscuttle, who simply hated cats. 'I shall soon deal with them! Or mice – ' She shuddered at the very thought of mice and hurriedly added "six mouse traps" to the top of her shopping list, before putting a kettle of water on to boil.

It was then that Miss Grimscuttle noticed something rather odd and out of place. Her table lamp was standing on the washing machine. When, in fact, it had absolutely no business being in the kitchen at all!

'Now how in the world did *that* get there?' she exclaimed irritably. She snatched up the lamp, which was rather a nice one with a carved wooden base and rose-patterned shade, and stalked back into the sitting-room to put it on the piano, where it belonged.

For the rest of that day Miss Grimscuttle worked very hard on getting Blackberry Farmhouse exactly how she wanted it. She put up flowered curtains and unpacked all her crockery. She made her bed and hung her clothes in the wardrobe. Then she fetched a hammer and some

long sharp nails and started knocking them into
the wall, ready to put up her pictures. Most of
the nails went in easily, but there was just one,
over the fireplace (where she especially wanted
to put her favourite mirror with a gold frame)
which behaved in a very unusual way. Every
time Miss Grimscuttle hammered it in, the nail
would suddenly pop out again. It happened three
times, very quickly, and with a tut of annoyance
Miss Grimscuttle took a deep breath and tried
once more.

After several good hard bangs, the nail seemed to stay where it was supposed to. But as soon as Miss Grimscuttle came back with the mirror, she found that the nail had vanished; and when she looked down, there it was, on the carpet. She picked it up and jabbed it angrily back into the little hole, but it flew straight out again. *Almost* as if somebody was on the other side of the wall, pushing it.

Miss Grimscuttle was furious at not being able to put her mirror exactly where she wanted it to go, but to save time she decided to try somewhere else. And this time, the nail stayed in. By bedtime Miss Grimscuttle was so tired that she fell fast asleep the moment her head touched the pillow. And it never even occurred to her to suspect that her bedroom was – well – not *quite* as empty as she thought it was...

Chapter Four

PHANTOM FOOTSTEPS

The next morning Miss Grimscuttle was awakened early by the sound of the telephone ringing. She hurried downstairs in her night-dress and curlers to answer it. But when she picked up the receiver and said 'Hello?' there was no reply.

'Brrrrrrrrrrr!' went the telephone, in a very cheeky way.

'Rats!' snapped Miss Grimscuttle, slamming down the receiver in a rage.

She stamped back upstairs and got dressed in her oldest clothes. It promised to be a lovely, sunny day and Miss Grimscuttle thought she would go and do some gardening. In fact, she could hardly wait to get started! The idea of pulling up all those horrid, tangly weeds made Miss Grimscuttle feel quite happy, and singing to herself she went to the kitchen for a quick breakfast.

On the way, she paused to look admiringly into the sitting-room, when a shriek of horror rose to her lips. It was unbelievable! *Everything* was in a different place! To start with, the table was upside down on top of the piano. And on each of the table legs a dining chair was precariously balanced, rocking back and forth in a most alarming manner. And the piano stool was standing on the writing desk with the television – oh my goodness, yes, the television! – dumped upon its seat. And higher still, on top of the television perched the table lamp with the carved wooden base and rose patterned shade.

As she stared, Miss Grimscuttle felt herself go pale. White as a sheet, in fact. For two whole minutes she stood and fumed; then she had just begun frantically wondering how on earth she could get everything straight again, when she heard the footsteps.

Miss Grimscuttle listened intently. They were going up the stairs. Yes, definitely up the stairs, because the third and seventh ones had a most distinctive creak. Creeeeeak, went the third stair as Miss Grimscuttle listened, holding her breath

with amazement and fury. Creeeeeaaaaak, went the seventh, and at that Miss Grimscuttle rushed out of the room. Whoever it was wandering about in *her* house, walking up the stairs as if they owned the place, making the telephone ring and playing circus tricks with her beautiful furniture, she would soon see *them* off!

Miss Grimscuttle thundered up the stairs in pursuit of the footsteps, and when she got to the landing she stopped, peering all round. There was nobody there.

'Hiding, eh?' she muttered, and started yanking open all the doors. First she looked in her bedroom.

'Come out!' she yelled. But nobody answered. Nobody appeared. And nothing moved.

'Come out!' she shrieked into the next room, which was empty; that is, except for an odd kind of little echo which said, 'Come out, come out, come...' Miss Grimscuttle slammed that door and opened another.

'I know you're here!' she roared. And the echo whispered, 'Here, here, here...'

After she had examined all the rooms Miss Grimscuttle stood on the landing, biting her nails in annoyance. There just didn't seem anywhere for that impudent intruder to hide, and Miss Grimscuttle was just wondering whether he (or she) could have sneaked down the stairs while her back was turned, when the footsteps started again.

Chapter Five

WHO'S THERE?

This time, they were right over her head. On the other side of the ceiling, in the attic.

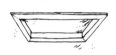

'Ah!' breathed Miss Grimscuttle, smiling a sly, satisfied smile. 'I've caught you now, my lad!' The big trapdoor was closed, and so high up anyway that Miss Grimscuttle knew she would have to stand on something to push it open. Her kitchen steps would do; she just had to fetch them from the little cupboard under the stairs, and then –

Clumpetty clump! Clump CLUMP! The footsteps got louder as whoever it was positively stamped on the trapdoor. Miss Grimscuttle ducked her head and scampered down the stairs, carefully avoiding treading upon the seventh and third steps. It would never do to let the intruder know her plan!

'Some old tramp, no doubt,' muttered Miss

Grimscuttle to herself as she quietly drew out the steps. 'Probably used to sleep in the house while it was empty, and thinks he owns it! Well, I'll soon teach him a lesson!' And, tucking the steps under her arm, she crept back up to the landing and opened them out beneath the trapdoor.

Bang, thud, wallop, STOMP! The noise was

getting louder by the minute. It began to sound like a whole army on the march! Miss Grimscuttle started up the steps and reached the trapdoor. She gave it a gentle push, but it didn't budge. She shoved harder. Still it refused to move.

Standing on the very top step, Miss Grimscuttle heaved with all her might and main but she could not dislodge the trapdoor. And in the end she had to fetch the coal hammer to loosen the edges. All the while she was hammering on her side of the ceiling, the footsteps were thudding about on the other, and it wasn't long before pieces of plaster started cracking off.

'At this rate, the whole house will fall down!' panted Miss Grimscuttle, wondering if she ought to stop. But just then, the trapdoor began to give, and with one last heave Miss Grimscuttle pushed it triumphantly aside. Grasping the sides of the trapdoor, she scrambled into the attic, and stared round.

There was nobody there. What's more, the footsteps had stopped the moment she had poked her head inside.

'Well I never!' gasped Miss Grimscuttle. 'And

where are the footprints? There is so much dust up here that there ought to be footprints all over the place. But there aren't any at all! Not a single one!'

There *were*, in fact. Two footprints. Large and flat. But they had been made by Miss Grimscuttle herself.

Having satisfied herself that the attic was completely empty except for a few spiders, Miss Grimscuttle climbed carefully down the step-ladder and went downstairs. Feeling dreadfully puzzled, she tucked the steps away. Then she hurried into the sitting-room, meaning to re-arrange *some* of her furniture at least. But with one foot over the doorway, she stopped and stared, unable to believe her eyes. Because everything had been put back again – exactly where it belonged! Every single thing was in its proper place, even the table lamp, which stood innocently on the piano as if it had never been anywhere else!

'That settles it!' announced Miss Grimscuttle in a loud and determined voice. '*Nobody* plays ducks and drakes with me in my own house! Now I shall most *certainly* send for the police!'

Chapter Six

CONSTABLE STARLING

Police Constable Starling came to Blackberry Farmhouse on his bicycle. And as he trundled down the bumpy, weedy path, he wished quite hard that he was going somewhere else. It wasn't that he was *frightened;* policemen never are. But he felt just a teeny little bit uneasy, because he had heard so many strange tales about the old house. And if there wasn't any truth in the stories, why had the last two owners left in such a tearing hurry? Fled for their very lives, in fact!

However, when Miss Grimscuttle came out to meet him, looking rather angry but otherwise quite normal, he began to feel a bit better.

'You are late, Constable!' snapped Miss Grimscuttle, as PC Starling propped his bicycle against the ivy-covered wall. 'This is a very serious matter, and I want it attended to, straight away!'

'That's what I'm here for, Madam,' said the policeman, and pulling off his bicycle clips he followed her into the hall.

'Now, what – ' began Constable Starling, taking out a notebook and pencil. But Miss Grimscuttle interrupted him.

'Just come with me!' she demanded. And leading the policeman into the sitting-room, she began to explain.

The more Miss Grimscuttle explained, the more Constable Starling wished he hadn't come. Or that his friend Constable Greengrass had been on duty when Miss Grimscuttle's telephone call came through. Or that he had taken that job up in Scotland last year.

Or that –

'So what are you going to do about it?' demanded Miss Grimscuttle as she ended her tale.

Constable Starling didn't know, but he would never have admitted it for the world. All the while Miss Grimscuttle was talking, he had begun to feel very peculiar, as if he was incubating something nasty, like the measles. He wondered if a rash had started to appear on his face yet. But when Miss Grimscuttle came to the bit about the footsteps, well, his hair simply stood on end underneath his helmet, and he knew for a fact that he hadn't got anything nasty at all. But Miss Grimscuttle had. Without a doubt, she had a g- a g- . The Constable stopped and tried again. The farmhouse was actually being h- ... It was no good, he could not bring himself even to *think* the words! And anyway, how could he tell Miss Grimscuttle? It wasn't right to go about frightening ladies who lived alone, even somebody as fierce as this one.

Constable Starling took out a big white handkerchief and mopped his brow. Then he pretended to search everywhere for Miss Grimscuttle's intruder, knowing all the while that it wasn't any use.

'Well?' demanded Miss Grimscuttle when he had finished. Constable Starling shook his head.

'I'm afraid I didn't find anything in the least suspicious, Madam,' he admitted.

Miss Grimscuttle scowled fiercely. 'Are you trying to tell me I imagined the whole thing?' she demanded, beginning to turn purple with fury. And before she exploded altogether, Constable Starling said soothingly, 'No, I'm not. But I

can't go arresting somebody who isn't there, can I?'

Just then, a terrible thing happened. *Somebody* tapped him on the shoulder. His left shoulder, actually. Twice. Tap, tap. Just like that. But when he turned round to look, the room was empty, except for himself and Miss Grimscuttle of course. And it couldn't have been her, because she had been standing in front of him all the time; without moving.

31

P.C. Starling decided it was time he went. In fact, he had just remembered that he must report back to the Police Station. Immediately.

'Wait!' screamed Miss Grimscuttle, as he made for the door. 'What are you going to do about this intruder who keeps dodging into my house and playing tricks...?'

But P.C. Starling was already on his bicycle, pedalling rapidly away. With a snort of annoyance Miss Grimscuttle stalked across the room and slammed the door.

Chapter Seven

MISS GRIMSCUTTLE'S GUESTS

Nothing else unusual happened for the rest of the day and Miss Grimscuttle had a lovely time pottering about in the garden, clearing out the toolshed and mowing the lawn. Later on that afternoon she decided to ring up some friends and invite them to visit her the next day, because she was so anxious to show off her lovely new house.

The telephone was behaving itself for once, and she got through straight away to Miss Peastocking, who was a schoolteacher in a little village called Hag's Ditch.

'Oh, it sounds perfectly lovely!' cried Miss Peastocking, when Miss Grimscuttle told her

about Blackberry Farmhouse. 'I should be delighted to come!' And so, it seemed, would Mrs Featherly and Mrs Gobowen and Miss Trickle and Miss and Mrs Cheeseman.

'That's enough,' murmured Miss Grimscuttle with satisfaction, beginning to make plans. 'Those two Cheesemans will eat as much as everybody else put together. Perhaps I shouldn't even have asked them; they are sure to ride over on their badly behaved ponies, and make great hoofmarks across my nice lawn. Still, never mind, it's done now so I'd better set to and get on with some baking.'

Before she went to bed, Miss Grimscuttle made a blackcurrant cheesecake and a mandarin cheesecake. Then she made two dozen sausage rolls and eighteen mince pies and fourteen vol-au-vents filled with strawberry jam and fresh cream and a chocolate gateau and eight eclairs and six meringues and fourteen ginger biscuits.

'There!' she said at last, standing back to admire with considerable satisfaction the mounds of lovely food. '*That* should be enough, even for those hungry Cheesemans! I'll do the sandwiches tomorrow.' She went to bed soon afterwards, and fell fast asleep straight away.

And it never even occurred to her to wonder if that slight *bulge* behind the curtain was caused by the wind, or whether it meant that somebody – or some*thing* – was standing there. Ever so quietly. Just…watching…

The next afternoon Miss Grimscuttle bustled about getting ready for her guests. First she put a snowy white cloth on the big polished table in the sitting room. Then she carried in all the fancy dishes she had made the night before, as well as a whole pile of sandwiches with assorted fillings, and a big bowl of lettuce and tomatoes and other salady things.

'Almost time,' said Miss Grimscuttle. And glancing at the clock she put the kettle on to boil, then sat down to wait for her guests.

The first to arrive were the Cheesemans. They galloped down the lane, through the gate, over the lawn, and pulled up outside the back door with a thudding of hoofs. As Miss Grimscuttle went to let them in, they jumped from their saddles and the ponies put their heads down and instantly started eating everything in sight.

As soon as the ponies had been tied up where they could do the least harm, Miss Grimscuttle

led the Cheesemans inside.

'Oh I say, Grim, what a super spread!' boomed Mrs Cheeseman at once, bits of straw and hay seeds springing out of her hair. 'You've certainly done us proud, old girl!'

'Just look at those marvellous cheesecakes!' cried Miss Cheeseman, secretly wishing she hadn't eaten *quite* so many chips that dinnertime.

'Do take a seat,' Miss Grimscuttle invited, 'while I go and open the door.'

She had just seen Miss Peastocking ride in on her bicycle, and almost immediately behind her came Mrs Featherly, having given Miss Trickle a life in her little red car. Miss Grimscuttle had already guessed that Mrs Gobowen, who walked everwhere, would probably be the last to arrive. She was. And then they were ready to begin.

Chapter Eight

A RATHER UNUSUAL PARTY

Everything went beautifully at first. Until they had finished the sandwiches and were about to start on the sweets.

'Now!' fussed Miss Grimscuttle, bustling in with a tray of fresh tea. 'What else would everybody like?'

'Cheesecake, please!' called Miss Cheeseman, who had only eaten eight sandwiches, so as to leave plenty of room.

'Certainly!' beamed Miss Grimscuttle, seizing a big, shiny cake slice. 'Which flavour do you prefer?' Actually, Miss Cheeseman preferred them both.

'Er – er – ' she said, hesitating as long as she dared in the hope that Miss Grimscuttle would say, 'have some of each'. But she didn't, so Miss Cheeseman said, 'Blackcurrant, please.'

Nobody could quite remember exactly what

happened next, but just as Miss Grimscuttle was
lifting up the cheesecake to place it in front of
her, it seemed to slip out of her hands and turn
upside down in mid-air, landing with a plop
right on top of Miss Cheeseman's head.

'You terrible old butterfingers, Grim!' roared
Mrs Cheeseman, snorting with laughter.

'Gracious me, how on earth did that happen?'
fluttered Miss Peastocking.

'Indeed to goodness, it looked as if it *flew*

across!' shrilled Mrs Gobowen.

'You've been at that cooking sherry again, dear!' teased Mrs Featherly.

'Wow!' breathed Miss Cheeseman, as the cheesecake dropped in big blobs over her cheeks, and sticking out her tongue she began to lick it up.

'I'll get a cloth,' panted Miss Grimscuttle in confusion, scurrying out to the kitchen. Somehow or other they got Miss Cheeseman cleaned

41

up and what was left of the cheesecake had to be thrown away. Then Miss Grimscuttle gave her some of the other one, this time leaving it firmly on the table while she dished out.

'Mrs Gobowen, I'm sure you would love an eclair,' said Miss Grimscuttle encouragingly, knowing that they were Mrs Gobowen's favourites.

'I'll pass them across to her, Grim,' said Mrs Cheeseman. 'You sit down, old girl. You've done quite enough damage for today!'

And with a hearty chuckle she seized the plate and offered the eclairs to Mrs Gobowen. They were absolutely beautiful; long and flaky and puffed with air. On top was a generous covering of milk chocolate, and inside each split was an oozy mound of fresh cream. Mrs Gobowen's eyes gleamed with pleasure.

'There's *lovely*, look you!' she breathed, and she reached out to take an eclair. And then the most terrible thing happened. As Mrs Gobowen stretched out her hand, five eclairs seemed to leap up from the plate and fasten themselves to her fingers and thumb!

Chapter Nine

THE TERRIBLE TABLE

'Aaaaaargh, get them off!' shrieked Mrs Gobowen. 'They're *eating* me!'

She leapt up, overturning her chair and jogging Miss Trickle's elbow so that the cup of tea she was drinking splashed on Mrs Featherly's skirt.

'Oh, my best dress!' cried Mrs Featherly, flinging up her hands in dismay. Unfortunately, just at that moment Miss Peastocking was passing the plate of biscuits to Mrs Cheeseman, and a blow from one of Mrs Featherly's flailing arms sent the whole lot flying across the room.

'Wow, it's raining biscuits now,' murmured Miss Cheeseman, as two fell into her second helping of cheesecake. And she scooped them up on her spoon.

Meanwhile, Mrs Gobowen's screams were growing more hysterical and Miss Grimscuttle

dropped the sugar bowl she was carrying and
rushed to her aid. Quick as a flash, she seized Mrs
Gobowen's wrist and pulled the eclairs from her
fingers, one by one.

'Oh, oh!' moaned Mrs Gobowen, sinking into
a chair. She sprawled across the table, cradling
her head in her cream-smeared hands. 'Oh, oh,

44

they were trying to eat *me*!'

'Stuff and nonsense, Gob,' said Mrs Cheese-man scornfully, biting into a crackling vol-au-vent.

'You just imagined it, dear,' said Miss Pea-stocking, sympathetically patting Mrs Gob-owen's arm.

'Your hand must have slipped accidentally,' guessed Mrs Featherly, returning from the kitch-en where she had been to wipe her dress with a tea-towel.

'Miss Trickle,' sang out Miss Peastocking, 'don't jog the table, dear!'

'I'm not,' said Miss Trickle indignantly.

Even so, the table seemed to give a little jolt, and Mrs Featherly had to make a grab at her tea-cup, which rocked in an alarming fashion.

'*Do* put your knees down, Cheese,' said Mrs Cheeseman to her daughter. 'You're lifting up the table that end.'

'I'm not, Mum,' said Miss Cheeseman.

'Well, *somebody* is!' declared Miss Grimscuttle, staring. And at that very second, the table de-tached itself from the floor and floated into the air.

'Oh, oh, what's happening?' shrieked Miss Trickle, leaping up.

'Push it down!' shouted Mrs Cheeseman, and they all tried. But the harder they pushed, the higher the table rose.

'Look out! The sausage rolls!' squealed Miss Peastocking. But it was too late. The rolls rolled right off the table and broke into bits on the carpet.

'The cheesecake!' gasped Miss Cheeseman, as the remains of her favourite dish slid off with a splurge, spattering itself all over Mrs Gobowen's feet.

'Watch the tea!' shouted Mrs Cheeseman.

'The milk – ' wailed Mrs Featherly as the jug waltzed across the table as if determined to upend itself in her lap. It did. In fact, the table tilted so high at one end and dipped so low at the other, that the entire contents shot off on to the floor. And for a few terrible moments the air was filled with the sound of crashing crockery, trickling tea and breaking biscuits. And, of course, the bewildered cries and screams of the guests.

Chapter Ten

PHANTOMS, SPECTRES AND SPOOKS!

The table didn't stop tilting until it was completely empty. Then it sank back to the floor, where it stood, still as a stone. All the ladies gaped down in horror.

'Oh my, just look at the *mess*!' gasped Miss Peastocking.

'Well, I hope nobody will blame me!' twittered Miss Trickle.

'*I* didn't do it either, Mum,' declared Miss Cheeseman, wondering if she dared scrape the least squashy lump of cheesecake from the carpet and –

'But I know what *did*!' cried Mrs Featherly, suddenly turning pale. 'Miss Grimscuttle, there is a strange and unusual presence in this room, something that enjoys making mischief – '

'Stop burbling, Feather, and explain,' suggested Mrs Cheeseman.

'She means a spook,' said Miss Cheeseman.

'A – a – a – phantom?' gasped Miss Peastocking.

'Or even a *spectre*!' nodded Mrs Featherly, staring wildly round.

'Spook? Phantom? Spectre?' shouted Mrs Cheeseman with a sudden snort of laughter. 'By golly, you've got a *ghost*, Grim!'

'GHOST?' shrieked Miss Peastocking, her eyes like two saucers. 'Oh – oh – er – I think it's

time to go home and feed my goldfish! Goodbye, dear Miss Grimscuttle, and thank you for a
lovely tea!'

And seizing her bicycle, Miss Peastocking
pedalled furiously away.

'I'm afraid I have to leave as well!' said Mrs
Featherly in hasty and nervous tones. 'To fill up
with petrol, you know. Before the garage
closes.'

'I'll come with you, Mrs Featherly!' gasped
Miss Trickle, fearful in case she should be left
behind.

'Ghost?' choked Mrs Gobowen, turning positively green. 'Indeed to goodness, I'm *terribly*

allergic to ghosts!' And without even saying goodbye, she fled through the door and down the path into the lane.

'Wow,' said Miss Cheeseman.

'Your grotty old ghost is a real spoilsport, Grim!' laughed Mrs Cheeseman.

'I don't believe in ghosts,' said Miss Grimscuttle. And instantly a large, ripe tomato rose from the carpet, whizzed across the room and hit her on the nose.

It took her the rest of the evening to clean up the mess. And that night she was utterly exhausted by the time she went to bed.

Outside, there was a big, bright moon and a smattering of stars. And if Miss Grimscuttle had stood in the garden and looked upwards, she might have noticed something very *unusual* sitting on her chimney pot. Laughing to itself.

'Ho-ho-hoo-hooooooooo!' it hooted. And the sound echoed down the chimney into Miss Grimscuttle's room.

'Those owls are noisy tonight,' murmured Miss Grimscuttle drowsily, as she dropped off to sleep.

Chapter Eleven

THERE'S SOMETHING IN THE CHIMNEY

There was something in the chimney. Miss Grimscuttle heard it first while she was having breakfast. A sort of faint scratching and scrabbling, which made Miss Grimscuttle put down her cup of tea to listen hard.

'A bird. A stupid bird,' said Miss Grimscuttle at last. And she waited for it to drop down among the ashes. But it didn't, and the sounds went on. In fact, the scraping, fluttering and scuffling grew louder and more frantic until it sounded as though not one bird, but a whole flock, were pecking and clawing inside the chimney, beating at it with great wings.

Bits of soot began to fall down, and Miss

Grimscuttle leapt up from the table in alarm. She rushed to the telephone and with trembling fingers, managed to dial the number of Mr Smith, the sweep.

'Hallo?' said Mr Smith.

'Oh, I'm so glad you are there, Mr Smith,' said Miss Grimscuttle hastily. 'I fear there is a bird – perhaps even more than one – trapped in my chimney, and I wonder if you could come and get it out?'

'I should think so, my duck,' said Mr Smith. 'What's the address?'

'Blackberry Farmhouse,' said Miss Grimscuttle. 'It's – '

'*Where* did you say? interrupted Mr Smith hurriedly, as if he couldn't believe his ears.

'Blackberry Farmhouse,' repeated Miss Grimscuttle, and just before he rang off Mr Smith had time to shout, 'Sorry, but I'm booked up till Michaelmas…'

'In that case,' snapped Miss Grimscuttle, furiously banging down the receiver, 'I suppose I shall have to do it myself!'

Squaring her shoulders, she strode back into the kitchen, then somewhat stiffly got down on

hands and knees upon the rug and peered up the
big chimney. She could see nothing. It was
absolutely black. And there was something odd.
All the sounds had suddenly stopped. As if –
well, almost as if whatever was inside the chimney, was looking down at *her*… waiting…

'That's funny,' said Miss Grimscuttle, and a kind of little shiver crept, very slowly, all the way down her back. 'If I were not such a sensible, level-headed and down-to-earth kind of person, I might almost start thinking it really *might* be a – '

She stopped and vigorously shook her head. 'That is total rubbish!' Miss Grimscuttle told herself severely. 'There are no such things as ghosts!'

And the next instant a whole pile of soot roared down the chimney with a whoosh and covered her from head to foot.

'Aaaaaaargh!' screamed Miss Grimscuttle, leaping backwards. She dashed towards the stairs, scattering soot everywhere. And just as she was passing the front door, somebody rang the bell. Thinking that Mr Smith the sweep might have changed his mind and decided to call on her after all, Miss Grimscuttle rushed thankfully to the door. She yanked it open to see two children standing there.

Chapter Twelve

STEPHEN AND ANGELA

'Excuse me,' said Stephen politely as soon as the door began to open. He had been about to say, 'I wonder if you could spare some things for the school rummage sale?' But when he saw Miss Grimscuttle – well – he couldn't help it. He simply stood and goggled. And Angela, his sister, who had come to help, froze to the spot with horror. She was too frightened even to scream! Because all those peculiar stories about Blackberry Farmhouse were true, after all! And there it was, a dreadful black monster with staring eyes and a round red mouth, swaying before them upon spindly legs!

It took several seconds for the children to realise that the monster was only a lady covered in soot. They were just beginning to feel a bit

silly for having been so scared, when they saw something else. Hovering in the air. Just behind her left shoulder.

Wide-eyed and open-mouthed, the children stared, and Miss Grimscuttle thought they were still staring at her.

'I'm afraid I can't stop and talk to you now,' she explained irritably. 'As you can see, I have had an accident with some soot, and I must – '

'Look!' gasped Stephen, being the first of the two to find a voice. He pointed into the hall, and Miss Grimscuttle spun round. There was nothing there.

'Look at what?' she demanded. 'Don't try and play jokes with me, young man. I must go and have a – '

'But it's *there*!' shouted Stephen. 'Angela can see it as well, can't you Angie?'

'I don't want to!' wailed Angela, covering her eyes with her hands and peeping fearfully through her fingers. 'Let's go, Stephen! I don't like ghosts!'

'GHOSTS?' gasped Miss Grimscuttle. Her eyes popped. 'Do you mean – there *really* is – where?'

'Just behind you!' cried Stephen. 'Over your head!'

'By your left ear!' squealed Angela.

'Looking over your right shoulder!' shouted Stephen. 'Floating near your hand!'

But it didn't matter which way Miss Grimscuttle twisted and whirled, or how quickly the children pointed and yelled 'There!' she could not catch the smallest glimpse of the elusive ghost. At last she gave up, exhausted. Leaning against the door she panted, 'Please – can – you – tell me – what it looks like?'

'It's white,' whispered Angela. 'With enormous black eyes! Ugh!'

'It keeps changing shape,' said Stephen, and they began to back away. 'But mostly it's like a great big flour sack with two round holes near the top – er – sorry, we have to go now! Goodbye!' And turning, they took to their heels and fled.

By now, Miss Grimscuttle was in a terrible state. She rushed into the sitting-room, still covered in soot from head to foot. She quivered like a jelly and sank down into her best armchair, not knowing, or caring, that she had made a big

58

sooty mark on the seat.

'A ghost!' gasped Miss Grimscuttle. 'So it *was* a ghost all the time! Moving the furniture! Making the telephone ring! Stamping about in the attic and up the stairs! Hooting down my chimney last night pretending to be an owl, and worst

of all, ruining my lovely tea-party! It must have been the ghost that Mr Slick, the estate agent, was trying to warn me about, but I didn't listen! Oh, oh, whatever am I going to do?'

And Miss Grimscuttle put her head in her hands and moaned. But not for long.

'I shall be able to think more clearly if I am *clean,'* said Miss Grimscuttle determinedly, and hurrying upstairs, she jumped into a lovely warm bath.

She scrubbed off all that awful soot and dried herself on a pretty pink fluffy bathtowel. Then she put on a blue dressing gown and orange slippers, meaning to change into her best clothes and walk down to the village.

'I shall buy a sponge cake filled with fresh cream and lemon curd, as a special little treat,' said Miss Grimscuttle. And, feeling almost happy once more, she went to open the bathroom door. But she couldn't. It was firmly shut. Tight as a clam. And the key wasn't there. Somebody – or some*thing* – had locked her in from the outside.

Chapter Thirteen

HELP FROM THE CHEESE-MANS

'Aaaaaaargh!' roared Miss Grimscuttle, flying instantly into a fearful rage. 'Grrrrr! Let me out, you horrid ghost! I know it's you!' She beat on the door with her fists, but nothing happened. The door remained closed. Miss Grimscuttle rushed to the bathroom window and opened it wide.

'Help!' she shouted. 'Help me! Somebody come!' But nobody was going past Blackberry Farmhouse just then. The lane was empty, and so were the fields. As far as she could see. Except for a scarecrow, who took no notice at all.

Miss Grimscuttle began to get cold. She stood by the window looking out and shivering for

what seemed ages. And at intervals she kept
trying the door, but it was no use.

'I can't stay here for the rest of the day!' said
Miss Grimscuttle through chattering teeth. 'I
must get out somehow!'

And she suddenly noticed the ivy leaves rust-
ling beneath the window sill.

'Ivy!' cried Miss Grimscuttle in delight. 'And it looks very strong! That's it, I'll climb down! It's sure to bear my weight!'

It did. Miss Grimscuttle crawled carefully out across the sill and clutching the ivy she climbed slowly, hand over hand, towards the ground. She was only halfway down when there was the clatter of hoofs outside in the lane, and the two Cheesemans pulled up their ponies and stared.

'Hallo, what the dickens happened to you, Grim?' shouted Mrs Cheeseman. 'Get locked in the loo, did you?' And they both laughed heartily.

Miss Grimscuttle gritted her teeth and scurried down the last few strands of ivy. Meanwhile the Cheesemans had galloped their ponies across the lawn to find out if they could help.

'It's that ghost,' explained Miss Grimscuttle miserably, clutching her dressing gown round her. 'It really is leading me a frightful dance. I simply don't know what to do!'

'Cunning little brutes, ghosts,' said Mrs Cheeseman sympathetically. 'Harder to get rid of than fleas on a hedgehog. You need somebody *really* clever – '

She broke off, suddenly. And Miss Grimscuttle wasn't absolutely sure, but she fancied that a strange gleam had sprung into Mrs Cheeseman's eye.

'I suppose you don't know of anybody?' asked Miss Grimscuttle, hardly daring to hope.

'I *might*,' said Mrs Cheeseman cautiously. 'But let's get you inside the house first, old girl. I mean, you are beginning to turn positively blue.'

As soon as Miss Cheeseman had balanced on her pony's back and climbed through the pantry window and opened the front door for them, Miss Grimscuttle and Mrs Cheeseman hurried in.

'Now,' said Miss Grimscuttle, 'please tell me the name of the person who can help me get rid of this ghastly ghost, and I'll go round there straight away.'

'It's a lady called Mrs Boffy, and she lives in Hag's Ditch,' said Mrs Cheeseman, speaking in tones which, for her, were unusually quiet.

'People reckon she's a witch!' exclaimed Miss Cheeseman brightly.

And no sooner had the words left her lips than the whole house seemed to go quite mad.

Chapter Fourteen

DEAR TEDDY

'W – wow!' stammered Miss Cheeseman.

'You idiot, Cheese!' shouted her mother. '*Now* look what you've done!'

'Oh my gracious goodness!' gasped Miss Grimscuttle, and the three of them clutched one another in alarm as objects of all shapes and sizes began whizzing about from room to room, flying through the air or trundling along the ground. They had to skip aside and duck very low to avoid being hit by hurtling cushions and spinning books, and even the contents of drawers spilled out to join the other things whirling overhead. More soot fell from the chimney and covered the hearthrug. Windows and doors rattled as if they were about to be wrenched from their hinges. And the sound of footsteps was like fifteen giants clumping up and down the stairs, while the telephone rang and rang, until it

seemed ready to burst.

'Stop it, stop it!' commanded Miss Grims-cuttle, reaching out to try and catch a pink and delicate shrimp plant as it flew past. But it dodged neatly away from her hand and went flying on.

'Quick, Grim, get dressed right away!' bawled Mrs Cheeseman. 'Mrs Boffy is your only hope, you know!'

'Stuff and nonsense!' snapped Miss Grims-

cuttle, grabbing at a cushion with no success. 'I
shall certainly not go and see this Mrs Boffy person! If there is one thing I do *not* believe in, it is
witches!'

And would you believe it, everything stopped! Not only stopped, but put itself back again
as if nothing had ever been out of place. In the
wink of an eye the whole house was tidy; there
wasn't even a single grain of soot left upon the
rug, and a lovely smell of lavender polish hung in
the air.

Soon after that, the Cheesemans left, hurriedly
galloping away on their ponies as if there were a
tiger snapping at their heels. But the rest of the
day was really lovely for Miss Grimscuttle, because there was absolutely no more trouble from
the ghost.

Perhaps it's gone to haunt somebody else, she thought hopefully, as she got into bed that night. Strange that it should have got into such a dreadful panic at the mention of Mrs Boffy. Anyway, it didn't seem to be in Blackberry Farmhouse now, so that was all that mattered.

Miss Grimscuttle snuggled down in bed and pulled the covers up round her ears, and it wasn't long before she began to fall asleep. And dream. It was really most peculiar. She dreamed about her old Teddy. He was pale golden brown with blue glass eyes, and he had the kindest smile you ever saw. One of his ears had frayed at the edge a bit, and there was sawdust coming out of two paws. But that hadn't mattered to Miss Grimscuttle. She had dressed him in a sweet little check shirt and some blue knitted overalls, and made a bonnet for when she took him for walks on cold days in her doll's pram.

Miss Grimscuttle smiled faintly, and shivered slightly in her sleep. It was rather cold now, actually, but dear Teddy would keep her warm. Here he came now, lifting a corner of the blankets ever so gently, getting into bed and snuggling up against her...There was just one thing,

though. One little thing was wrong with her dream about Teddy. Because Miss Grimscuttle had given Teddy away to her young niece, years and years ago. And yet – she could actually feel his cold little paws…touching her neck…and if it wasn't Teddy, then who – ?

'Eeeeeeeeee!' shrieked Miss Grimscuttle. She leapt out of bed and plummeted through the door and down the stairs and fell into the big armchair. Then she wrapped herself in a large tablecloth and pulled her knees up to her chin. And she sat there, shivering, for the rest of the night.

Chapter Fifteen

MRS BOFFY IS AT HOME

Every Midsummer, a fair was held on the Green at Hag's Ditch. And this time, Mrs Boffy was going with her young friends Ben, William and Mary. She was very excited because it was simply *ages* since she had been to the fair, and they had promised to take her on the Dodgem Cars. So when the doorknocker banged and Mrs Boffy hurried to answer it, no wonder she felt disappointed when only a tall, scraggy-looking lady stood there.

Bother, thought Mrs Boffy. But aloud she said politely, 'Can I help you?'

'Is Mrs Boffy in?' asked the scraggy lady hurriedly, and without stopping to wait for an answer she added, 'My name is Miss Grimscuttle.'

'Ah. Yes,' said Mrs Boffy. 'I am Mrs Boffy.'

'Really?' exclaimed Miss Grimscuttle, staring

at her in surprise. 'You don't look much like a
w-'
She stopped suddenly, and Mrs Boffy noticed
that, as she spoke, Miss Grimscuttle kept glancing all round her in a furtive, hunted kind of way.
As if she was afraid that somebody – or some-
thing – might be following her.

'I have a problem,' said Miss Grimscuttle.

'Oh dear,' said Mrs Boffy, thinking, what a nuisance! She really didn't have time for problems just then. The children would be arriving at any moment. But Miss Grimscuttle looked so worried that Mrs Boffy couldn't help feeling sorry for her.

'Please come in,' she said.

Once inside Buttercup Cottage, Miss Grimscuttle gazed curiously all around Mrs Boffy's cosy little parlour, then she said stiffly, 'It is not at all what I expected.'

'Well,' said Mrs Boffy mildly, 'it isn't *every* witch that likes to live in dank, dark, smoky, smelly caverns full of spiders, bats and toads, with a cauldron bubbling over the fire. However, I am in rather a hurry, so if you wouldn't mind...'

'Yes, I'm terribly sorry,' said Miss Grimscuttle hastily. 'I will come to the point straight away.'

Taking a deep breath and clutching her handbag very tightly, she said, 'I am being haunted by a ghost.'

'Ah,' said Mrs Boffy. 'Odd things, ghosts.

72

They vary, of course. Some can be got rid of quite easily. But others, well – ' she shook her head. 'It all depends on the type, and how long it has been on the premises.'

She raised an enquiring eyebrow and Miss Grimscuttle said desperately, 'I really don't know. But there have been rumours – '

'I see,' said Mrs Boffy. 'And what is its speciality? I mean, does it rattle doors and windows, or ring bells, or move furniture, or howl down the chimney, or play practical jokes, or make footsteps, or touch you with icy fingers – ?'

'Everything!' cried Miss Grimscuttle.

'Deary me,' said Mrs Boffy. 'That's the worst of the lot. But all we can do is try one thing, and if that doesn't work, have a go with something else.'

She went out of the room and came back seconds later with a dark green, strangely-shaped bottle in her hand. It had a very long neck and a bulgy, round base. Pushed firmly into the top was a big cork, and fastened to the bottle was a label covered with curly, thin writing.

'This is usually an excellent cure,' said Mrs

Boffy. 'But remember, you must follow the instructions *exactly*.'

Miss Grimscuttle was so anxious that she quite forgot to say 'thank you'. Seizing the bottle, she pushed it into her handbag and hurried out of the door.

Chapter Sixteen

THE BOTTLE

The first thing Miss Grimscuttle did when she returned to Blackberry Farmhouse was read the label on the bottle Mrs Boffy had given her.

It said, 'Stand in a cold, dark place. Shake the bottle. Three times at midnight. Quickly remove the cork.'

'Oh,' said Miss Grimscuttle, disappointed. She looked at her watch. It was only eleven o'clock in the morning. She did a quick sum in her head, and groaned. 'Thirteen hours to midnight,' said Miss Grimscuttle miserably. 'I only hope that nothing else awful happens before then!'

But nothing did. It was just as if the ghost knew all about her visit to Mrs Boffy, and was watching, waiting and listening, to see what she would do.

'The pantry should be cold enough,' said Miss

Grimscuttle, carrying the bottle there very carefully. She placed it under the bottom shelf on the stone floor, in the draughtiest corner she could find. Then she closed the door firmly and went outside to work in the garden until evening came.

Miss Grimscuttle could hardly wait till midnight. She tried to watch television but couldn't concentrate, and in the end she switched it off. Then she tried to do some knitting, but kept dropping stitches all over the place. Then she tried to read a book, but after going over the same page nine times without knowing what it was all about, she threw that down as well.

'I'll go and do it *now*,' muttered Miss Grimscuttle, standing up impatiently. 'It's nearly midnight, after all. And seven minutes can't make all that much difference. I'll get a spoon. I only hope the medicine doesn't taste nasty.'

Sorting out the smallest spoon she could find in case it did, Miss Grimscuttle fetched the bottle and trudged back into the sitting room. She shook the bottle vigorously, several times. Then she tussled with the cork, but it wouldn't budge. What was even more strange was the fact that the

bottle seemed to be quite empty. Funny she hadn't noticed it before! And anyway, how could she be expected to take three spoonfuls of medicine if the horrid stubborn cork wouldn't come out?

Panting with rage, Miss Grimscuttle pulled and tugged as the hands of the clock crept closer to midnight. And she was sure that she heard someone – or some*thing* – laughing, ever so quietly.

'Oh, oh, I shall never get it open in time!' cried Miss Grimscuttle. 'Only two minutes to go, and the cork simply refuses to move! Oh, oh, somebody help! HELP!'

Hardly had she spoken than there was a soft, whooshing sound and a figure shot out of the chimney to stand on Miss Grimscuttle's hearth-rug in a mist of soot.

'Mrs Boffy!' gasped Miss Grimscuttle. And she was so delighted that she didn't even notice Mrs Boffy's pointed hat. Or broomstick.

'You really should get your chimney swept, my dear,' said Mrs Boffy, brushing her skirt and shaking the soot from her cloak. 'You looked so upset this morning that I thought I would just pop in to see how you were getting on.'

'Oh Mrs Boffy, it will never work!' groaned Miss Grimscuttle. 'I can't even get the cork out!'

'Of course you can't!' said Mrs Boffy crisply. 'Remember what I said? You must follow the instructions EXACTLY. Now, read them again. And hurry! We haven't much time!'

Chapter Seventeen

THE PRISONER

'Stand in a cold place,' read Miss Grimscuttle aloud. 'But I did! It was in my pantry all – '

'No, no, not the bottle!' said Mrs Boffy. 'It means *you*. Now come on, there isn't a moment to lose!' And with Miss Grimscuttle leading the way, they rushed to the kitchen.

'In you go!' ordered Mrs Boffy, opening the pantry door just as the grandfather clock began to strike twelve. And Miss Grimscuttle obeyed; she scrambled inside to stand, shivering, upon the stone floor, squashed between shelves full of pickles and rice and baked beans and bottled fruit and apple pies and pizzas and home-made jam.

'Good. Now for the next bit,' said Mrs Boffy.

'Shake the bottle three times before midnight,' read Miss Grimscuttle. 'And it's nearly midnight now!'

'Dong!' clanged the big clock for the ninth

79

time as Miss Grimscuttle shook the bottle up and down; three times exactly. 'Dong! Dong! Dong!'

'Last of all,' said Mrs Boffy, ' "Quickly remove the cork." '

Gathering all her strength, Miss Grimscuttle gave the cork an enormous wrench. But she need not have worried. Because this time, it came straight out, plop! As easily as picking a daisy. Then the whole house went quite MAD.

The kitchen was suddenly filled with a rushing, roaring sound as if twenty-seven hurricanes were passing through. The cups and saucers rattled and danced upon the shelves and the saucepans swung frantically back and forth upon their hooks. The curtains billowed out and the cupboard doors banged open and shut, open and shut. The whole room seemed to be vibrating like a road drill, and they were almost deafened by a hideous, wailing screech.

Miss Grimscuttle longed to put her hands over her ears. But she couldn't, because she was having to hold on so tightly to the bottle, which was twisting about in her fingers as if trying to get away.

'Hold on tight!' shouted Mrs Boffy. And Miss

Grimscuttle did. With her arms aching and her hands sore and her feet numb with cold, she hung on. Then, quite suddenly, everything stopped. The wind ceased to blow. The cups and dishes became perfectly still. And the whole house was calm and quiet, just as it should be on a moonlit night in June.

'Quick, the cork!' hissed Mrs Boffy.

With trembling fingers, Miss Grimscuttle pushed back the cork.

'Look at the bottle,' said Mrs Boffy.

Miss Grimscuttle gazed down at the bottle; then she gave a gasp. There was something inside. Something which drifted and floated, spiralling, turning around. Something white, giving the green glass a milky look. And Miss Grimscuttle wasn't absolutely sure, but she thought she could see, near the top of the whiteness, two tiny black holes...like eyes...

'Is it the ghost?' gasped Miss Grimscuttle.

'Yes it is,' nodded Mrs Boffy with satisfaction. 'That spell worked beautifully, didn't it?'

She held up the bottle and gazed at it, thoughtfully.

'All that remains to be done is to find another home for the ghost,' she said.

'Another home?' echoed Miss Grimscuttle in surprise. 'But can't you just – well – drop it into the middle of the ocean? Or bury it in a deep hole?'

'Oh no, I could never do that!' cried Mrs Boffy, askance. 'Ghosts need a place to haunt in the same way as people need somewhere to live! Besides,' she added sharply, 'if the bottle should ever get broken, the ghost would fly straight back here and start haunting *you* all over again!'

Well of course, when Miss Grimscuttle heard that, she was only too pleased to leave everything to Mrs Boffy, and limped away to get some lovely woolly bedsocks for her stiff, chilly feet.

Grasping the bottle firmly, Mrs Boffy caught up her broomstick, leapt astride, and zoomed up the chimney, skywards to Hag's Ditch.

Chapter Eighteen

THE GHOST HOUSE

Mrs Boffy knew there was no time to be lost. She also knew exactly where she was going and what she was going to do. It was Mary, Ben and William, actually, who had given her the idea. She would never have visited the Midsummer Fair without them, but in the company of the three children she couldn't remember when she had enjoyed herself so much.

They had bobbed up and down on the round-about horses; they had whirled round and round on the Whizz-o-Chairs. They had shied at coconuts, and without using any magic at all, Mrs Boffy had knocked one down! They had spun hoops at the Hoop-la and Ben had won a blue china dog. They had wandered about with their faces buried in pink candy-floss. But best of all, they had crashed round in the Dodgem cars, taking it in turns to drive; William and Mrs Boffy

in one car, Mary and Ben in another, sparks
flying overhead, flags fluttering and everybody
screaming their heads off with delight as the cars
collided. Oh, that had been such fun!

And they had done something else.

With a swish of her cloak, Mrs Boffy brought
the broomstick gently to rest in the dark, de-
serted fairground. She looked up at the building
in front of her. It was made of huge pieces of
wood which would be quickly dismantled and
put together again when the fair moved to
another town next day. It was a most peculiar
shape, with crooked windows and bulgy walls,
and twisted chimneys and broken doors. The
outside was covered with scary paintings of
dancing skeletons, menacing spiders and howl-
ing spooks, and the sign on the top said 'GHOST
HOUSE'.

'Ghost House my foot,' said Mrs Boffy softly,
as she approached the doorway. They had gone
inside, William, Ben, Mary and herself. And –
well – there had certainly been some strange
effects, with skeletons popping out of cup-
boards, pretend cobwebs touching your face,
curtains blowing, and some awful shrieking

noises. But there had been something missing.

'There's nothing like the real thing,' said Mrs Boffy, stepping inside the house. Everything was still and quiet now, because the fairground generators had been switched off. Mrs Boffy lifted up the milky green bottle, and gently eased out the cork.

87

For a moment, nothing happened at all. Then suddenly, something white started to squeeze slowly from the neck of the bottle, like a thread of steam. It began to grow and grow, until a great, dense cloud of whiteness just hung there, staring down at Mrs Boffy with enormous black eyes.

'It's all right,' said Mrs Boffy. 'You're free now. Be happy.' And she spoke a small, magic word, which made the bottle disappear.

At that, the ghost flew with a wail of delight down the dark passage, to investigate its new home. And smiling to herself, Mrs Boffy got on her broomstick and jogged gently back to Buttercup Cottage, under the stars.